**LEMON
DROP
BOOKS**

www.lemondropbooks.co.uk

THEA LEMON
AND HER SUPER SPORTY
FAIRY GODMOTHER

By Mark Lemon
Illustrated By Maia Walczak

Published by Lemon Drop books

I would like to tell you a magical story about an ordinary girl named Thea Lemon. Thea lives with her Mum and Dad in a large city called Bristol in

England. Her parents own the Lemon Drop Café
on Church Road in St. George.

The café gets so busy that every weekend Thea is sent to stay with her terrible Great Aunt Fellulla, who Thea secretly calls 'Craggy Bottom'. Great Aunt Fellulla has curly blue hair, wonky round spectacles, and yellow teeth. She wears brown dresses and dirty black boots. She is known by the people in her village as the kind of person who never smiles, doesn't like Christmas and is always complaining about something!

Now let me get to the story, as there is quite a
story to tell. It was a frosty Friday afternoon
in December, and Thea's school bell had rung

to mark the end of the week. Thea and her friends
gathered in the school playground to talk about
what they were doing that weekend.

Thea's class were going to France for a very special two-day skiing trip. This was an extra-special treat as the children were going to watch the Super Spectacular Ski Slalom World Cup.

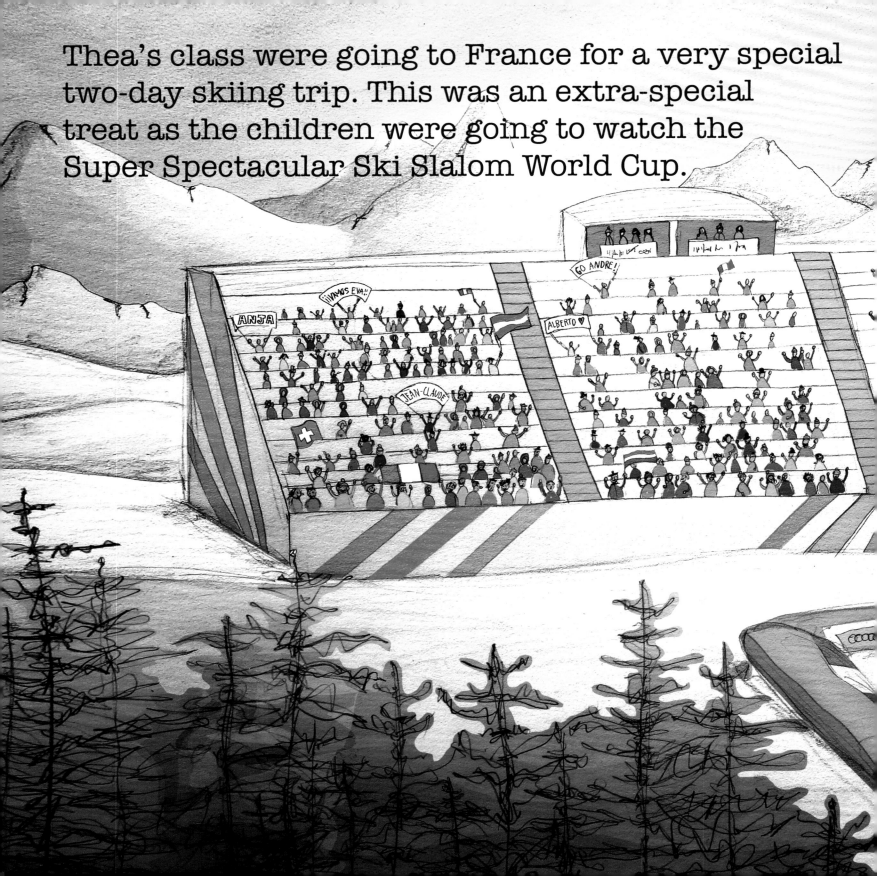

Sadly, Thea's parents couldn't afford to send her on the trip so instead she had to spend the weekend with her terrible Aunt Fellulla.

Thea's best friends, Susan Sillyman, Victoria Villington and Mary Millington were all talking very excitedly about the trip. Thea tried to be excited for them but when she left her friends she felt a little bit sad.

She went home to pack her bags for her six o'clock train.

Thea arrived at Temple Meads station and boarded her train. Her mum had made her favourite sandwiches: ham and cheese with sweet pickle.

Thea's train chugged along, through the small, pretty English towns and villages.

Finally, the train arrived into Haddenham and, as usual, Aunt Fellulla was nowhere to be seen at the station platform.

Thea picked up her bags and slowly made her way to Cabbage Cottage.

When she arrived, she got her key out of her bag and opened the large, creaking door.

"Hello? Aunt Fellulla, are you there?"
shouted Thea.

"Yes Thea, I'm in the living room. Now take your
bags straight up to your room, I have some chores
waiting for you!" bellowed Aunt Fellulla.

Thea went upstairs, sat on her bed
and looked out of her window. She
thought about all the fun her friends
were going to have at the Spectacular
Ski Slalom race the next day.

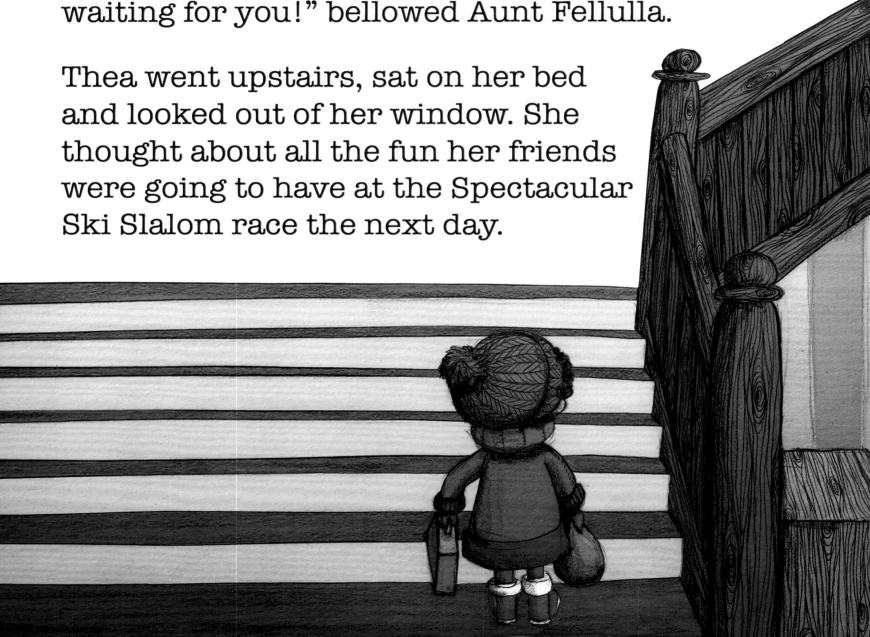

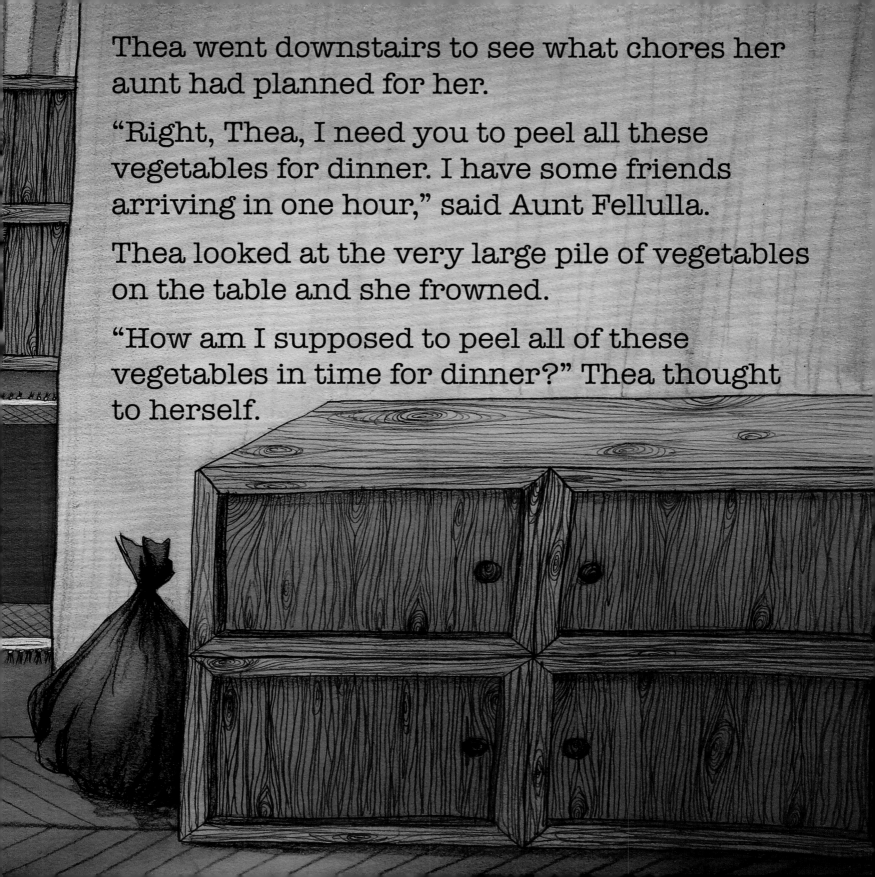

Thea went downstairs to see what chores her aunt had planned for her.

"Right, Thea, I need you to peel all these vegetables for dinner. I have some friends arriving in one hour," said Aunt Fellulla.

Thea looked at the very large pile of vegetables on the table and she frowned.

"How am I supposed to peel all of these vegetables in time for dinner?" Thea thought to herself.

Her hands ached from peeling so many vegetables. Thea was pleased to be allowed to eat her dinner in the kitchen with Sprogget the cat.

After dinner, Thea felt quite tired and went straight to bed, wishing that she could be on the way to France with her friends right now.

In the morning, Thea woke up having dreamed of being at the skiing event. "I so wish I could be at the Super Spectacular Ski Slalom World Cup right now," Thea said aloud to herself.

All of a sudden, there was a bright flash of light that seemed to come from her wardrobe. A little afraid, but mostly curious, Thea walked over to it and opened the door very slowly. There was another bright flash of light, which made her jump backwards and land in a heap on the floor.

Thea looked up and saw the most beautiful lady she had ever seen.

"Hello, I'm Serena, your super sporty fairy godmother!" said the lady.

She waved her glittering wand in the air, sprinkling sparkles everywhere.

"I'm here to make your wish come true."

Looking down, Thea realised that the fairy godmother had transformed her pyjamas into a new super-cool ski outfit.

"WOW! Thank you, Fairy Godmother."

"You're welcome Thea. It's time to go now."

"Go? Go where, Fairy Godmother?" asked Thea.

"Why, to the Super Spectacular Ski Slalom World Cup, of course."

Thea's Fairy Godmother waved her magic wand once again:

"With a swish of my wand,
away we go.
Come on, Thea,
we are off to the snow."

All of a sudden, both Thea and her fairy godmother found themselves standing on the side of a very large mountain with lots of snow.

Thea looked around and realised that she was standing next to her favourite ski champion, Lars Van Speedington.

"Hello, Thea. I'm very much looking forward to racing you today. Your Fairy Godmother has told me lots about you," said Lars Van Speedington.

"Erm, you have heard lots about me?"
Thea asked, her eyes wide.

"Oh yes! All of the top ski champions have heard of Thea Lemon," answered Lars Van Speedington as he adjusted his goggles.

Standing along the mountainside were hundreds of ski fans holding large signs to cheer on their favourite ski champions.

"Right, Thea, let's get you ready," said her Fairy Godmother.

"Get ready, Fairy Godmother? What for?" asked Thea.

"To race Lars Van Speedington, of course."

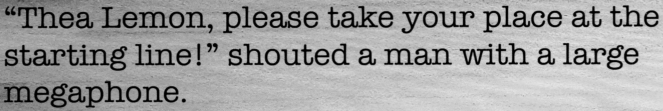

"Thea Lemon, please take your place at the starting line!" shouted a man with a large megaphone.

"But Fairy Godmother, I can't ski," said Thea, feeling afraid.

"Take your place at the starting line and wait and see, Thea," answered her Fairy Godmother with a smile.

Thea's tummy fluttered as she grabbed some skis and poles and took her place at the starting line.

"Five, four, three, two, one – GO!" shouted the man.

Thea and Lars Van Speedington both WHOOSHED down the mountain as fast as the eye could see!

Thea could hear the crowd screaming her name.

"Come on, Thea! Go go go!" shouted the ski fans.

"I'm winning the race!" she thought, looking over her shoulder to see Lars behind her.

A minute later
Thea WHOOSHED
past the finishing line,
winning the race!

Thea could see her best friends, Susan Sillyman, Victoria Villington and Mary Millington, all waving and cheering.

"Look girls, it's Thea!" shouted Susan.

"She's beaten Lars Van Speedington!" shouted Victoria.

"Well done, Thea!" shouted Mary.

Thea was presented with the Super Spectacular Ski Slalom World Cup, while all the fans cheered her name.

She felt like the most special girl in the world.

"Well done, Thea. It's been lots of fun, but now we must get you home," said her Super Sporty Fairy Godmother.

Thea's Fairy Godmother waved her wand three times, saying these magical words:

"With a swish of my wand,
away we go.
We must return,
to the place we call home."

Both Thea and her Fairy Godmother found themselves once again in her bedroom at Cabbage Cottage.

With a wink to Thea, her Super Sporty Fairy Godmother stepped into the wardrobe and with a flash of light she was gone!

That night, Thea was the happiest girl in the world. She dreamed of her Super Sporty Fairy Godmother, skiing with her hero, Lars Van Speedington and winning the Super Spectacular Ski Slalom World Cup.

Goodnight!

ACKNOWLEDGEMENTS

Thank you to my beautiful daughter Thea for the inspiration for this story. You are my star in the night sky!

It wouldn't have been possible to bring this story to life, if it wasn't for the amazing illustrations by Maia Walczak. Thank you for doing such a brilliant job.

Big thanks to all the proof readers for casting their talented eyes over the story.

The final product wouldn't have been possible if it wasn't for Doveton Press Printers, Bristol.

Finally, I would like to thank my family – Simone you have been a continued support whilst I have been through this process, I love you very much! And Otis and Thea for the continued inspiration to create new stories.

Very special dedication to Dad - James Lemon

'You walk with me always'